ESCAPE

Emilia Mitch

Contents

Prologue

I am walking down an aisle surrounded by people and nature. I hear people chanting "All hail the princess!" As I reach the end of the aisle, a tiara is placed on my head by a middle aged Man who has similar sets of wings as mine. The top of my wings are white but changes to silver towards the end. Everyone is wearing royal attire and have wings too but with different shades of colours. I feel as if I belong there.

*****

I am jerked awake from my sleep by my blaring alarm that reads 5:30 am. I am not at all in the mood of going to school but it's the only way I can get to meet my friends. I creep out of my bed and enter the bathroom to start with my daily routine. As I'm putting on my hijab I remember about the dream I had moments ago. This is the third time that I have seen this dream in a span of a month. The setting is the same but the scenario in all three dream's were different. When I had seen this dream for the first time my heart was ripped out while I was walking down the aisle. The second time I was stabbed with a dagger multiple times in my abdomen while walking down the aisle but the third time when this very dream occurred I was not at all attacked. "How strange!", I muttered to myself. After having my breakfast and making sure that I have packed all my books for the day, I left for school.

The entire day went on as lengthy and mundane as usual but the thought of those absurd dreams were constantly showing up in my mind like those irritating advertisements that love to flash out after every few minutes on the internet. I saw my side table alarm beaming 9:00 pm so I decided to get ready for bed. Once I got comfortable in my bed, I was immediately overcome with sleep due to the great amount of homework that was given to us today by various teachers. As I drifted off to sleep I hoped that those dreams don't occur again!

____

Chapter 1

"Hey, have you seen the latest news trending on Instagram?", Shahid asked me chirpily.

I immediately frowned on hearing the word Instagram since my phone has been confiscated by my parents and I'll be only getting it back a week later.

"Shahid!! Did we not agree on not talking about anything regarding phones?", Leila scolded him.

Shahid and Leila are my best friends and we have been together since kindergarten. "I don't know what I will do without them", I thought to myself. These two feel more like family to me than my own family.

"Are you guys still coming with me to the library?", I asked the both of them.

"Obviously!", They both said together while Leila gave me an expression that showed she mentally facepalmed.

*****

"Finally I can now get some work done, but the two of you can't go a minute without bickering." I retorted at my friends.

Leila and Shahid had been arguing about some petty thing that went viral on the internet. Man, these two are always at each other's necks, that the thought of how they even become friends still bothers me!

"Yeah let's go in and get rid of those books sis!", Shahid encouraged me.

Shahid is a type of person that doesn't believe in fantasies and happily ever afters. He thinks that if you can't see anything in reality then it doesn't exist, so you can see he is not really into much about fantasies! I on the other hand can't even live a second without fantasizing regarding anything and Leila well... She is more of the inbetween.

"Are we even going to enter or just stand out here and stare at the walls?" Leila deadpanned.

I have been visiting the towns local library for the past 8 years and never have I felt anything strange but today feels different. As we entered the library a feeling of malevolence stirs within me. I feel as if something terrible is going to happen.

"Hello Mrs, Collins. How are you this fine afternoon?", I greeted her as usual.

"Hello children, I'm doing just fine.", She greeted back.

Mrs Collins has been working in the town's local library way before I even moved here. She is a really sweet and kind lady.

"Oh, Ayanna I see you have come for more books. The latest additions have just arrived, hold on let me get them for you from behind the counter.", She informed me.

As we stood by the counter for Mrs Collins, I scanned the shelves packed with books from one corner to the other of the library hoping that my eyes will lend on something interesting and fortunately it does. I spot something glowing on a shelf just to the right of the counter.

" What is that Mrs Collins?", I asked her curiously.

"Which one?", She asked as she came out of the counter with a stack full of books.

"That one over there on the top left of the shelf that looks like it's gonna fall out any minute!" I said while pointing towards the book.

"Oh, that old worn out book!", Mrs Collins replied with a sad look.

Leila immediately grasped the book and read it's title "The legend of Angels and Jinns". Hmm, I have read many books about all sorts of legends but this one sounds very different and the most absurd thing is that I sense an aura coming from it. How does it even have an aura, not that it's alive, but still how is it possible that something such as a book that is not living have such a strong aura? This is absolutely absurd!

I leave the book alone and get back to Mrs Collins about the stack of latest addition books that just arrived. Mrs Collins has always admired my fondness towards reading books hence she makes sure that I get to read all the interesting ones first and therefore keeps them aside for me for my next visit. I quickly return the ones I borrowed last month as I checked the time on my watch telling me that it's almost 4:00 pm and that I better leave as soon as possible or else I'll be scolded yet again by my mother. Argh, why do parents have to be that strict!

As Leila, Shahid and I get seated in the car to leave with a stack of 6 latest addition books for me to indulge myself in, the thought of the book that I spotted reappears in that over curious mind of mine and I rush back to the library to get it.

"Wow, what was that about? If you left something in you could have atleast told us before running off like a wild goose!" Shahid said concernedly. He likes to play the role of an overprotective friend.

"Sorry, I couldn't help myself with all the curiosity running wild in my brains!", I apologized and they both laughed back at me as if I just cracked a joke.

*****

I arrived home late yet again and to my dismay I had to brave myself for another scolding again. Why is it that I'm always scolded when I arrive late but my siblings aren't when they arrive late. That is so unfair!

I left the books on my study table and went downstairs for dinner. We all ate in silence. After we finished have dinner I helped my mother with the dishes and thereafter left to my room to retire for the night. As I was changing in to my PJs I remembered about the weird vibe that I was getting from that book. It was as if I share some kind of bond with it, but I let the thought pass by so that I could sleep peacefully or else I would waste the entire night thinking about it. With that I got into bed and effortlessly drifted off to a sweet slumber.

Chapter 2

It has been two days and that malevolent feeling is still there. I wonder what is causing those unsettling feelings to arouse within me ever since I visited the library on Wednesday.

"Girl, you have been staring at that book for the past two hours!", Leila remarked.

"Well what do you suggest I do, because those unsettling feelings are eating my insides!" I retorted back.

"I suggest that you should open that book and see what lies within it.", Leila suggested.

"But I fear something terrible is going to happen and that fear is growing intensely!", I exclaimed.

"Well you can't just sit idle and expect your answers to be handed to you on a silver platter, now can you!" Leila said encouragingly.

"I fully agree with you on that" Shahid said supportively as he entered with a large box of pepperoni pizza and a bottle of Coke.

"What on earth took you so long to arrive?", I asked him.

After begging my parents for the umpteenth time they finally agreed on allowing Shahid and Leila to come for a sleepover but even with that I have to obey to certain conditions. Conditions that every Muslim family dishes out to their daughter when there is a male friend that is going to visit whether it is her friend or her siblings.

"Well what do you think took me so long, when there is a Circus Carnival in town?", Shahid asked as if we were oblivious of what is happening in town.

"Oh yeah the Circus Carnival, that completely slipped out of our minds!" Leila said as the thought of the Carnival settled within her.

"So what are we gonna do on this fine Friday night?", Shahid asked with a smug look.

"Let's play true or dare!", Leila immediately responded back.

"Oh boy, I hope this doesn't go the way I think it will!", I thought to myself. Whenever we play truth or dare Shahid always makes Leila or I do something weird that often results in a huge embarassment.

"Bingo!", Shahid immediately exclaimed.

"Ok then bring that food here so that we can eat while we are playing this game.", I ordered them.

Leila poured Coke for all of us so that we can use the half empty bottle to spin. After we all settled down on my blue fluffy rug, we began the game. Leila was the first to spin the bottle and as the bottle slowed down it landed on Shahid.

"True or dare?", I asked him.

"True!", He immediately chose trying to play it safe.

"Ok, then why is it that you constantly call me sis, not that I mind you calling me that but you never call Leila that?", I asked him.

"Well, do you remember that incident that happened with my parents and you defend me...", He started with.

"Mhmm...", I said as I recalled the incident.

"I always wished for a sister but never got one till that day when you defend me as if you were my sister, so from there on I started respecting and seeing you as my sister. Hence I mostly call you sis.", He finished of with.

"Awww...", Both Leila and I reacted with.

"But what about me?", Leila asked.

"Well, that's another story for later...", Shahid trailed off with a sheepish look.

He spinned the bottle while taking a bite of his slice of pizza. Unfortunately the bottle had to land on me and they both quirked with excitement.

"True or dare?", Leila asked this time.

"Dare!", I chose boldly.

"Hmm, I dare you to open that book you found in the library and read the first page!" Leila ordered me.

Oh boy, why did I have to be that bold, now look what I got myself into. She is making me do something that I haven't braved myself to do for the past two days.

"Okay...", I said as I gulped while glancing at the book.

I quickly got the book and set down to continue with Leila's ridiculous dare.

"The Legend of Angels and Jinns." I recited the title of the book.

As I opened the book a blinding white light escaped from it causing me to surrender to the darkness of my mind. Before I completely drifted away I remembered the three of us being stirred away to Allah knows where.

*****

Chapter 3

U nknown POV

"What in the name of Angelea was that?" I asked myself.

I have been living in Neráides from the time I was born which was 30 Supermoons ago and never have I witnessed someone enter through the gates of Spectral let alone a thing.

"Mother did you see what happened?" I asked mother.

"Yes child, it seems that three foreigners have entered Neráides through the gate of Spectral." Mother replied with astonishment.

"Foreigners, is that what you seem mother!", I asked bewilderingly of the term used by mother.

"Yes child, foreigners!", Mother repeated.

"But mother how is that possible, the gates of Spectral have been locked from centuries?", I asked as more curiosity sparked within me.

"Well child, in the name of Angelea all shall be known within precise timing.", Mother informed.

In the name of Angelea I hope time flies by like the speed of wind in a blizzard and soon shall all be revealed to the people of Neráides.

Hi guys!

Short bonus chapter and welcome to Neráides. You must be wondering what and where Neráides is but like I said all shall be revealed within precise timing. Also what do you think will be revealed to the people of Neráides? Till next time folks

Sam

*****

Chapter 4

As I seeped out of my darkness I was immediately hit by the fragments of my memory. The book from the library. A blinding white light escaping out of it. Leila, Shahid and I being stirred away by the white light.

On realising about Leila and Shahid, I immediately jerked awake but was hit by an immense pain in my head at the same speed.

"Leila, Shahid, where are you?", I asked my surroundings.

"Morning child, it seems you have awoken.", Greeted a middle aged woman.

"Who are you and where am I? Where are my friends?", I asked panicky.

"Easy there child! I am Pheona, one of the best healers in Neráides and your friends are being resided in the nearby chambers for proper care and treatment. You can go and visit them later in the day when the pain in your head subsides!" Pheona informed me.

"Neráides, what and where is that?" I asked curiously.

"Oh child, in the name of Angelea you sure are a curious one! Why don't you rest and when you and your friends are fit all shall be explained!", She said like a mother nurturing her young ones.

"But what about my friends, how are they doing and where are their chambers?", I asked worriedly.

"In the name of Angelea, your friends are doing fine. The female one is kept directly besides your chamber on the left and the male one is kept opposite of you chamber. They are not held too far away from you, child.", She said in a sarcastic tone.

"Rest now, child and in the name of Angelea all shall be explained by the High Lords.", And with that she left.

As she left, my curiosity immediately quirked and I rewind all that she had said in my mind. "Neráides, where is that?", I thought to myself. I have never heard of it and this Pheona lady... She has wings just like that of a fairy. They were as shiny as glitter starting of with white at the top and with a faint of cerise pink towards the end. Speaking of Pheona why does she always say "in the name of Angelea" . Who is Angelea and why is she regarded with so much importance.

Oh Allah what have I gotten myself and my friends into. "Leila, Shahid, I hope you two are doing fine and are safe. I will come and see you as soon as I get rid of this pain in my head." I muttered to myself.

As I thought more and more about Shahid, Leila and where that white light might have stirred us to, Neráides and the way Pheona looks I hadn't realised that the pain in my head had increased. My head was now throbbing immensely wanting me to surrender to a hypnotizing slumber that was constantly calling out to me. I closed my eyelids to be consumed by the sleep in the hope that my friends are well and that I will get the answers to my invisible questions...

Hi guys

Ayanna has escaped her darkness but only to be welcome into Neráides. What do you think of Pheona and who is Angelea? Will Ayanna get the answers she is prying for? Till next time folks.

Sam

*****

Chapter 5

I was revived back to reality from my sleep by a series of thuds on the door which I assumed to be knocks. As I rubbed off the remaining sleep that was still left in me a boy slipped in through those swinging doors. He looked as though he was still in his youth years some where between the ages of 24 and 27 and just like Pheona and the other creatures like her that I had seen, he too had wings. As usual his ones also started with white at the top and changed to an ocean blue colour towards the tips of the bottom part of the wings. Man, what are these creatures? Are they fairies? Are they Angels? I asked my mind.

"Hello, you must be Ayanna?", The boy asked.

"Yes, that's me and you must be?", I asked him back.

"I'm Luke, and was sent her to give you a fresh pair of clothes and there after take you to the eating hall.", He informed me.

"Oh okay, and I apologize for the tardiness!", I said in pure embarassment.

"Well that's ok and in the name of Angelea you do not need to apologize." He said bluntly.

"Oh, here goes the in the name of Angelea" I muttered under my breath.

"Well then could you show me where I can bathe and change?", I asked him since I had not seen any other doors in the room besides the ones through which Luke entered.

"Oh uhm, just move that table over there and a door will appear. You can bathe and change in there.", He informed me.

"Well then see you in a bit!", I exclaimed.

"Okay, I will be waiting outside for you and your friends to change.", He said and with that he left to wait for us.

I did as he said and being true to his words a door immediately appeared as I moved the light weighted table that was lying in the corner of the room. As I entered the invisible room I was instantly rendered speechless at how poshish it looked. I removed my clothes and immediately started with what I had come to do. Once I was done I left to head to the eating hall and again being true to his words, Luke was waiting outside and within seconds Leila and Shahid also appeared from their rooms. All four of us then headed towards the eating hall following Luke's directions.

When we entered the eating hall both Leila and Shahid's eyes including mine turned the size of dinner plates at the enormous amount of food that was placed. Instantly our stomachs growled and we realised how hungry we were. When we were done dishing for ourselves and had settled down to a nearby table that was vacant Leila and Shahid started conversing among themselves.

"Well, since you all are fit now Head Healer Pheona ordered me to escort you all to the Royal Castle!" He said.

"The Royal Castle!!", Both Leila and Shahid quirked.

"Yes, the Royal Castle. You all are foreigners here and do not know how the people of Neráides live, hence you are being escorted there.", He said.

"Uhm, before you take us to anywhere can you tell us what you are and why you have wings?", I asked.

"Very good question, we the people of Neráides are Angels and hence we have wings but the colour of our wings differ with each family.", He informed us blatantly.

"Neráides, where is that?", Shahid asked curiously.

"Hold a second, did you just say Angels, could this mean that the white light that came out of that book swallowed us into it since it's title had something to do about Angels!", Leila said panically.

"I'm not sure of that, only the Lord knows the answer to that and about Neráides I will tell you all about it on our way to the Royal Castle.", He said confusedly.

"Ok, then when do we leave for the Royal Castle?", I asked.

"We leave immediately once you all are done feasting.", He said.

"Then what are we waiting for, we need to leave this place as soon as possible!", Shahid said with new enthusiasm.

"Alright then, Head Healer Pheona has packed everything for us and since you all can't fly a carriage has been arranged for.", He said with excitement.

With that we all got ready to leave for the Royal Castle unaware of the dangers that will ly in our path.

Hi guys

So finally we now know what those winged creatures are. What are your thoughts on Luke? Do you think that the assumption that Leila made is true? What dangers will ly in their path? So many questions to which the answers are still unknown! Till next time folks.

Sam

*****

Chapter 6

"So you are saying that Neráides is the land of Angels and...", Shahid repeated Lukes words.

"Yep and there are other lands also which I will tell you about later." Luke said while cutting off Shahid.

"What there are other lands too, is this like a whole different world?", Leila asked in utter surprisement.

"More like a realm." Luke answered and corrected her at the same time.

"So what's with the whole in the name of Angelea thing?", I asked in an attempt to subside Leila's excitement.

"Angelea is the long lost princess of Neráides, who was taken away for her safety to another realm 17 moons ago during a brutal war. After the war was over the Lord sent groups of warrior Angels to different realms to look for her but none succeeded. Due to that all started to assume that she might have not survived and died therefore she is given outmost respect and is regarded as a God.", Luke narrated.

"Are you sure that the warrior Angels were sent to all the realms what if they missed one and she could still be alive?", Leila asked as though doubting Luke's words.

"Moons...", Shahid mused before Luke could answer to Leila's curiosities.

"Moons are used to calculate time and 1 moon is a year.", Luke replied flatly.

As we continued to bombard Luke with questions trying to ease our curious minds we heard a sound.

"Wow, did you hear that?", Shahid asked panically.

"Yep, that was pretty loud we all heard that.", Leila said as if it was nothing to be worried about.

As we traveled the sounds grew louder forming into those created when swords clash against each other and within seconds after, a piercing growl was heard causing everything around us to shake as though an earthquake occurred.

On hearing that piercing growl Luke immediately stopped the carriage and we all stepped out of it to inspect what the source of that growl was and to our dismay we had to be spectators of a gruesome and horrific scene. In front of us laid a scene that looked as though it was taken out straight from a fantasy but then again both my friends and I were already stuck in a fantasy world about which we didn't even have the slightest clue about, so what are the odds. There in front of us was another Angel, a creature wearing a black hooded cape and a very horrifying creature that looked like a wild dog but with 3 heads and about 13 feet tall.

"Oh Allah, what is that creature?", I asked while being both terrified and amazed.

"That is a Cerberus, one of the dangerous creatures of the Zehraal forest that can only be controlled by a Jinn.", Luke answered.

"So is that black hooded thing a Jinn?", Shahid asked.

"Oi, are you guys just going to stand and watch this thing kill me or are you going to help me defeat it so that we can get out of this forest.", Shouted the Angel that was still fighting the Cerberus.

"We've got to do something. We can't just let him be killed by that mons ter.", I said trying to encourage the others to help.

We all agreed to help and with the other Angel's directions we managed to injure the Cerberus causing it to retreat back to where it came from. Due to that the Black hooded creature which Luke said was a Jinn also vanished.

"Oh Allah, you are injured gravely.", I said as I took in the features of his body.

"It's nothing to be worried about and thank you for saving my life.", He said.

"There is a first aid kit in the carriage, it would be enough to patch you up.", Luke informed the other Angle.

"Thank you all for your kind service, I owe you my life.", He said.

"You welcome, but that is not needed.", I said flatly.

"Why not, a life for a life. I Damien Salvador the fourth, Commander of the Royal Warrior Angels vows to serve his life for you and your fellow comrades.", He immediately vowed to me.

Once we got Commander Damien who looked too young to be a commander all patched up, we settled back in to the carriage to head to the

Royal Castle before something or should I rather say someone caught Shahid's attention and it was none other then my other best friend, Leila.

"Hey, where is Leila?", Shahid asked.

"Oh Allah, don't tell me that we lost Leila!!", I said both panically and worriedly.

Hi guys

Another cliffhanger and Ayanna finally knows about Neráides and the history behind the whole in the name of Angelea thing. Yet again she has made a new friend and what do you think about Damien? Will he hold up to his vow? Where do you think Leila is? Is she lost or is she kidnapped? Till next time folks.

Sam

*****

Chapter 7

W e have been looking for Leila for the past 3 hours and still we have no clue about her whereabouts. I hope that what I had feared of does not occur.

"It's starting to get dark and it's not good to travel through the Zehraal Forest during the night", Commander Damien informed us.

"But what about Leila, we have to continue looking for her!", Shahid said while being over worried about Leila.

"We know but we can't stay in this forest for long. We need to look for a cave or a save place for the night or else we will be devoured by the monsters of the Zehraal Forest.", Commander Damien said is if he was too familiar with the forest.

"There up towards the north is a cave, it should be save enough to stay for the night.", Luke said while pointing towards the cave.

We all agreed to head towards the cave that looked as though it would take us eternity to reach. As we traveled, I couldn't help myself from steeling glances at the Commander. Never in my life have I ever been attracted to a male but something about Commander Damien feels weirdly sinister but in a good and fascinating way at the same time. It feels as though two different people with opposite qualities were merged together. "Oh Allah, why am I being attracted to him?",, I asked my subconscious mind.

As I was about to glance at Commander Damien once again I felt as if I saw something move from the corner of my right eye. No, I must be paranoid! First I enter a magical realm that I have no clue about and now one of my best friends is lost. Yeah that's it, I must be paranoid with all these changes and stress.

"Hey there's the cave, we have finally reached.", Shahid said exhaustedly.

We all quickly made our way into the cave and with the flick of a finger Luke created a torch. Wow, they can do magic I wonder what else they can do! As we scanned the cave with the help of the torch I started hearing faint breath's coming from the far left of the cave. I wonder what it could be. Oh Allah, I hope it's not another horrifying creature!

"Can you hear that, it sounds like faint breath's coming from there.", I whisper to Shahid while taping his shoulder trying to show him the direction from where it's coming.

"Yeah, I hear it too.", He whispered back as we moved closer to the sound.

As we got closer to the sound with Luke and Commander Damien trailing us, I immediately gasped as the flickering lights of the torch fell on something that looked like the silhouette of a girl. Shahid looked back at Luke and gestured him to lower the torch to see what it actually is. As he did so we all were shocked when we saw who it was. I felt the ground beneath me twirling my brain like a furious tornado and my guts churning in the most disgusting way that I can't even imagine of. "Who could have done that to her?", I thought as anger boiled within me. There lying in a pool of blood with bruises covering almost every part of her body was my best friend Leila. Shahid and I immediately ran to her with tears spilling from our eyes.

"Leila, Leila, wake up?" Shahid said while shaking her body to wake her up.

"Water, water..." She whispered exhaustedly.

Commander Damien immediately flicked his fingers and a bottle of water appeared. I snatched it from his hands and quickly opened the cap while tilting it towards Leila's mouth and she gulped it down ferociously.

"Who did this to you?", Commander Damien asked.

As Leila lifted her head in an attempt to answer him her face completely changed from relief to scared with bits of fear looming in her eyes within seconds as though she saw a horrific creature lurking behind us and before I could even turn around I felt as if I'm being sucked into a vacuum. I feel suffocated and I'm instantly greeted by darkness and the everlasting fear looming inside me.

*****

As I regain my consciousness I groan feeling the pain seeping into each and every bone and muscle of my body. Once the pain has relaxed I slowly flicker my eyes trying to adjust with the amount of light surrounding me but to my disappointment it's pitch black but when I look around I notice that there is a faint glow of light emitting from me. It looks like it's engulfing me. I use the light coming from it to see where I am and it seems as though I'm in a cell or a dungeon. I immediately start to search for a weapon or anything with which I can get out of here and while I was doing so sounds of foot steps started to echo towards my direction.

"Well, well, what have we here..."

Hi guys

Cliffhanger!! What do think of the state in which Leila was found? Who do you think was behind Ayanna and her friends in the cave? What do you think has happened to them and why is Ayanna in a cell/dungeon? What do you think is causing that faint glow around her? Yet again we have unsolved mysteries! Till next time folks.

Sam

*****

Chapter 8

On hearing those footsteps and the way they were getting louder with every step caused me to freeze in my spot. "Oh Allah, who could that be and where are my friends?", I asked myself while being terrified of the worst possible scenario that could occur.

Suddenly the footsteps stopped and a screechy sound escaped booming throughout my surroundings and with that a dreadful feeling began to settle within me.

"Well, well, what have we here...", Said someone with a very strong but gentle masculine voice.

On hearing that my brain quickly jump started to figure out who's voice it could be but to my dismay nothing came forth. Who could it be and where is everyone else, Shahid, Luke Commander Damien and Leila? Oh Allah Leila, she was brutally injured!

"It seems we have got our hands on an Angel. Hmm, how interesting!", Said the same person as he laughed away at my situation.

An angel who is he refering to because I am not one and I don't seem to see anyone else here but then again it's pitch black over here and the only source of light is the one that is engulfed around me.

"Who are you and why have I been kept in here? Where are my friends?", I asked the invisible Man since I could only hear him and not see him thanks to the lack of light.

How I wish I could see who this invisible person was and on the thought of that the glow around me suddenly got brighter. How did that happen? I'm just an ordinary human, I don't even have any powers and nor am I an Angel! How do I always end up in a dilemma? Firstly I don't know where the glow of light engulfing me came from and suddenly it has now brighten!

"Now, now, Angel no need to panic there!", He said with a sadistic smile that I was able to get a glimpse of and with that he decided to step closer causing me to gulp in utter fear of what he might do.

As he got closer to the cell, the glow of light around me allowed me to get a better view of who this invisible person is and on seeing him I felt like emptying my guts out and returning back to my darkness but unfortunately I could not do so since I needed answers. Answers of my friends whereabouts! Answers of how I even got into this realm in the first place! Answers of too many invisible questions! Whoever this person or creature is since there hardly is any Humans around looks scarry and dreadful. He has black veins running all the way up to his neck and h-his eyes are c-completely b-black. "Oh Allah, please just get me back to my home!", I begged in my mind in an attempt that Allah may hear my plea and a miracle occurs.

"Oh you poor little Angel, I'm Gythe and you are being kept held in Thirío the land of Jinns.", He said in a booming voice and that snarky laugh.

"I'm not an Angel and why have I been kept here. What wrong have I done?", I remarked trying to hide away my fear.

"You seem to be a fearless one but how naive of you. You think you can fool me! You reek off fear and that is what makes you even more delicious.", He said sadistically.

"You ask what wrong you have done? You being an Angel itself is a great mistake and now I will feed on your fear and devour you.", He continued in the same booming and sadistic tone.

On hearing myself being devoured by him my knees nearly gave away and tears began to seep through my eyes. Hold on, I am not an Angel then how can he devour me?

"I am not an Angel! I do not even belong to this world. I was sucked into this realm of which I have no knowledge off then how am I an Angel?", I asked being utterly annoyed at being constantly referred as an Angel.

"It seems you are more naive then expected! Have you not given any knowledge of the fact that any Angel who enters Thirío has a glow around them and this is one of their greatest weaknesses.", He informed me as blatantly as though even a baby would know of such information.

I-I am an A-angel! H-how? Is that why I was able see the glowing book? Is that why I was seeing those dreams? Oh Allah those dreams, they made me feel as though I belonged there! As I got more and more seeped within the confinements of my brain searching for clues and answers I was suddenly brought back to reality by a loud bang.

Hi guys

Just as Ayanna thought that she has escaped a dilemma she is instantly thrown into another and this time she is thrown into Thirío the land of Jinns and Gythe. What do you think of him? Along with that she has discovered that she is an Angel. How do you think that happened? What invisible questions is she talking of to which she needs answers? What do you think of Ayanna's assumptions? Oh I almost forgot, above is an esthetic of Gythe do check it out and let me know your thoughts. Till next time folks.

Sam

*****

Chapter 9

Bbbbbooooommmm.

Just as I thought that I was completely drowned within the depths of my brain searching for clues and answers I was brought back to reality by a loud bang. This caused me to wonder who or what it could be completely distracting me from what Gythe said. I moved my gaze from the floor of the dungeon towards where the bang came from and while doing so I got a glimpse of Gythe's flustered face. This caused me to flinch away since his features were already frightening me due to those black veins and his black eyes.

"Ayanna are you there?", Asked someone whose voice felt oddly familiar.

"Ayanna, Ayanna, is anyone there?", The same person asked again but this time I was able to recognise who it was.

Commander Damien, is he here to rescue me? Where is the others? Are they save? I was about to reply to Commander Damien but before I could Gythe covered my mouth with his hand in an attempt of stopping me from uttering anything. Unfortunately he was not able to succeed as I kicked him where the sun doesn't shine causing him to groan in pain. It's funny how people always mistaken me as someone weak!

"Commander Damien, I'm over here just follow the glow of light!", I screamed at the top of my lungs so that he would be able to hear me.

"Ayanna is that you that is glowing?", He asked being astonished at my new appearance.

"Yes, it's me please be careful there is a Jinn over here!", I replied to him.

Commander Damien was able to reach me safely without being noticed by anyone else. He hit Gythe on his neck causing him to fall unconscious and put some kind of a spell on him so that he doesn't become an obstacle in our path. With that Commander Damien quickly opened the dungeon freeing me from it's dreadful confinements. We stealthily left the dungeon so that we don't get caught by another Jinn.

"Where is Shahid, Leila and Luke?", I asked him since I didn't see any of them with him.

"They are safely waiting for us outside the castle and before you start worrying again they are absolutely fine.", He said in a stern voice as though he was regretting us ever meeting in the Zehraal Forest.

"What about Leila, she was brutally injured?", I asked him even though he just told me not to worry about them but how can I not.

They are my friends and the only family I have in this unknown realm which I guess I am now a part of after what Gythe disclosed to me. On remembering Gythe's words I looked at Commander Damien and realized that he was not glowing. This made me curious as to why he was not glowing but then again Gythe could have been messing with my mind, so I decided to ask him about it later when we get to the others.

"Leila is doing fine, Luke has healed her with his powers.", He informed me with a hush tone.

*****

"Ayanna, Commander Damien, is that you guys?", I heard Shahid asking as though he was expecting us to show up sooner or later.

"Yes, it's us.", I replied to him in a hush tone, still feeling scared that some Jinn will come and capture us again.

On hearing that and seeing us, Shahid and Leila immediately ran and glomped me causing me to lose my balance and fall to the ground. Luke also appeared with his mouth open being absolutely surprised at my appearance since both of us were glowing.

"You are an Angel?", He asked still being in a state of shock.

"I-I g-guess I am one now. I-I don't know!", I replied to him staggeringly since I, myself wasn't aware of it until Gythe explained.

"H-how is that p-possible? You are from the human realm than how?", He asked as though he was not ready to believe what his eyes were showing him.

"I don't know! I also found out about it a while ago from Gythe and I'm still trying to process all that has just happened.", I said as I broke out into tears.

"Who is Gythe?", Commander Damien asked demandingly.

"He was the Jinn that you knocked out in the dungeon.", I told him while I was still crying.

Leila immediately came to my side and hugged me trying to somehow comfort me. Speaking of Commander Damien I remembered that I had to ask him why he is not glowing like Luke and I so I looked at him and braced myself to ask him.

"Commander Damien you are an Angel too but how is it that you are not glowing like Luke and I?", I asked him in an attempt that he might have a reason to it.

"I am a Commander of the Royal Warriors for a reason. I have been trained to hide my glow for such purposes since we Angels know it is one of our biggest weaknesses.", He informed us but I don't know why I felt as though he was somehow lying and hiding something from us.

"Okay!", Is all I could say since I was extremely exhausted from what happened to us earlier and all the information I had to process.

"We are still in the territory of the Jinns we need to leave Thirío as soon as possible or else we could be captured again.", Luke said with worry lacing his words.

We all agreed with him and with that we started to head out in to the unknown once again praying that we don't get anymore obstacles in our way.

Hi guys

It's my Birthday today so I decided to do an early update.

Ayanna has managed to escape from the claws of Gythe with the help of Commander Damien and has reunited with her friends. It seems that Gythe's words were true after all of her being an Angel but how? Well, that's still an unsolved mystery! Do you think Commander Damien is hiding something about his identity? Ayanna and her friends sure have started to head out of Thirío praying that they don't face anymore obstacles in their way but little do they know that this is just the beginning. Till next time folks.

Sam

*****

Chapter 10

We had decided to head out of Thirío but since we all were exhausted from the previous incidents, we settled on resting for some time and immediately leave at the break of dawn since it was already quite late.

"So what now you're an Angel?", Shahid asked.

"I don't know, cause although I'm glowing like Luke I don't have wings and nor do I have any magic or powers!", I replied to him while stating the obvious.

To be honest I'm still in a dilemma, not physically but mentally. My thoughts feel as though they are waging a war inside my mind. I don't know why I feel as though all the clues and pieces are right there infront of me but yet I'm unable to put anything together. I'm unable to complete this puzzle that my mind is trying to create. Unable to see the bigger picture if there even is one.

"You must be tired from what happened earlier, you should rest we will talk about this later.", Shahid suggested in an attempt of not over worrying me.

"Yeah okay.", I said in a meekly tone.

How am I suppose to sleep after what has happened. What if another Jinn comes and kidnaps us again! No, I will not let that happen again especially not after how Leila was attacked and injured. "Oh Allah, please give me the strength to overcome these troubles and protect my friends.", I mentally begged him hoping that he will listen to my prayer.

*****

"Ayanna, Ayanna, wake up we need to get going!", I heard Leila who I guess was nudging my shoulder.

I weakly pushed her aside and started rubbing my eyes and stretching. Hoping that will do the job and get rid off any remaining sleep.

"Aahhh, what time is it?", I asked feeling embarrassed if I might have over slept.

"Morning, Sleeping Beauty it's almost sunrise!", Shahid replied.

"Sunrise! Weren't we suppose to leave at the break of dawn?", I asked while thinking why we are still here.

"Yes, we were supposed to but someone decided to over sleep and not budge at all up until now, so we decided to wait!", Commander Damien replied in an irritated tone.

"Sorry.", Is all I could say back feeling embarrassed.

How could I have slept for so long and when did I even fall asleep. I remember my brain being on the verge of a war thanks to all those questions and events running around like a wild goose up there. I was so preoccupied in trying to put all those pieces together and find some kind of an explanation to what is happening to me that I didn't even realize when I surrendered to the night and fell asleep.

"I guess we should get going, staying here any longer will only bring more trouble!", Luke stated and I took that as my cue to leave this retched place.

*****

We were all walking in silence until Shahid and Leila decided to sneak up on me.

"So now what, you are going to leave us?" Leila suddenly asked almost giving me a heart attack.

"Wow, you almost scared the living soul out of me!", I exclaimed being surprised by her sneak move.

"No, who said so and why would I leave you?", I replied back while think about her question.

"Well, you are an Angel...", She trailed off with

"Firstly I'm not even sure if I am one, I agree I was glowing like Luke but other than that what proof do we have that I'm an Angel. Secondly you and Shahid are my only family here and I consider you guys as my siblings, so how can I leave you two. In fact you two are my world, there's no fun without you guys.", I immediately snapped at her.

On hearing that Leila instantly hugged me with tears in her eyes and Shahid also joined. Guess what, group hug! When we separated all eyes were on us. Commander Damien and Luke were staring at us with an expression of what's going on written all over their face.

"Uuhhmm....", I trailed off.

"Just continue walking!", Commander Damien said with his eyes shooting daggers at us.

Oh boy, and with that we continued walking. Shahid, Leila and I kept on talking about the previous incidents with me taking glimpses of the view and how the forest looks. We had been talking for so long that I hadn't even realized that other than us the forest was dead quite. No insects crawling here and there. No birds chirping even the leaves on the trees were as still as a statue. Shrugging it off I returned back to the conversation but before I could say anything my eyes landed on something intriguing. It was a very tall tree that looked like a face of a person was carved into it.

"What's that it looks like a face a person was carved into it?", I asked while walking towards it.

"Wait, don't touch tthhaatt...."

Hi guys

Another cliffhanger! So what do you think about Ayanna's thoughts? What puzzle has her mind created that she is desperately trying to complete? Do you think she will be able to put the pieces together and find out her real identity? What do you think that tree is that Ayanna spotted and why is she being told not to go towards it? Till next time folks.

Sam

*****

Chapter 11

- -

Commander Damien's POV

After seeing Ayanna's appearance in Thirío I was left astonished with millennium questions brewing a storm in my head as to how she is an Angel. Ever since I laid my eyes on her in the Zehraal Forest where she had saved my life, I had a feeling that she was different from her friends but I never expected this. How can a human that does not even belong to my world turn out as one but then again we are still not sure if she even is one. In fact even after being so close to the Royal Family for so many years and being the Commander of the Royal Warrior Angels, I am unable to decipher if a human is an Angel. I am unable to tell if this creature is a part of my people or not but at the same time I can tell if one is an Angel or a Jinn within seconds. I believe I have no option but to let time show case the truth unless Ayanna is She. She who my eyes have only witnessed being mentioned in a prophecy that lies in the most sacred place of the Royal Castle in Neráides. The prophecy which states:

LOST IS SHE IN THE DEPTHS OF THE UNKNOWN WORLDS

WHO SHALL RETURN TO CLAIM WHAT IS RIGHTFULLY HERS

BONDING SOULS TOGETHER WITH THE STRENGTH OF BOTH KINDS

IS SHE WHO SHALL RULE OVER EVIL AND GOOD

This very prophecy got me thinking if Ayanna is She who is being mentioned off. I have been trying to connect Ayanna with this unknown yet familiar prophecy that I myself don't believe in, is true. Since the day I was asked to see this unforetold prophecy by the King of Neráides I have been prying for it's meaning and significance. But unfortunately I have not succeed in doing so till date. Oh in the name of Angelea what dilemma have I been dragged into! "Angelea", and with that I feel myself slowly bit by bit surrendering to the darkness that I dread will one day be my worst outcome.

*****

I was awoken by the warm rays of sunshine seeping through the forest telling me that it's the break of dawn. Once I was rid of any remaining sleep in me I noticed that the rest of them were still sleeping soundlessly except for Luke who was sitting under a tree looking as though he was in some kind of a deep thought. I stood up to head towards him but before I could even reach him he looked in my direction acknowledging my presence. After sometime of talking with Luke we decided to go and wake the others up since it's not safe staying here. Luke woke Leila up and I did the same to Shahid and thereafter Luke told Leila to wake Ayanna up who didn't budge for a good couple of minutes. By the time we were all awake and ready to leave it was already past sunrise.

*****

We were walking in silence with Luke besides me and Leila, Shahid and Ayanna ahead of us until I heard Ayanna shouting "Group Hug". They were all embracing each other and when they separated and saw the confusion plastered on both Luke and my face I was intrigued in what happened but since I had no clue of what all that was I only said "Just continue walking." They all gave a sheepish look and turned around to continue walking.

After some time I heard Ayanna asking "What's that it looks like a face of a person was carved into it" while pointing to a tree and moving towards it. Once I registered what she was pointing towards it didn't even take me a second to figure out what it was but perhaps in her eyes I was already too late.

"Wait, don't touch tthhaatt...."

Before I could even finish that sentence she was already in front of the Ent. Ents are tree monsters who dislike being awoken from their sleep. They are very sensitive creatures but lack the skill of hearing things. They feel and observe what is around them.Although they are extremely patient and a cautious race but waking an Ent from it's sleep is a sight one wouldn't even imagine being in.

I saw Ayanna stroking her hand on the surface of the Ent's bark and before she could continue with her actions I immediately stopped her but what happened next made me feel rooted in my position. I saw the Ent opening its eyes and blinking a couple of times to adjust its eyes to the light.

"Who dared to awake Treebeard the Oldest Ent of Ents that exist from it's slumber?", It asked in a loud roaring tone.

"It was I and I apologize for doing so..."

Hi guys

At last we have something that is not from Ayanna's POV. Wow, what a twist have we here! Well what do you think about Damien's thoughts and the prophecy? Do you think Ayanna is she who is being mentioned off? What darkness is Damien speaking of that will one day be his worst outcome? What do you think of the Ent and what can you predict will happen next? Till next time folks!

Sam

*****

Chapter 12

I was walking towards the tree that got me fascinated about it when I heard Commander Damien scream "Wait, don't touch tthhaatt....", but unfortunately in my eyes it was quite too late.

My hands were already scanning the texture of the tree. The bark felt smooth but also rough at the same time. It felt as though the tree was not just a tree but a living, walking creature. Even the slightest touch can tell the amount of energy flowing within it. On realising the amount of energy running a marathon within the tree something within the cells of my brain clicked, putting two and two together. This instantly made me feel how bad of an idea it was to come towards this tree and perhaps the fact that Commander Damien just swatted my hand away from the tree might be a confirmation to the realisation that just dawned upon me seconds ago.

As I was about to reprimand Commander Damien for his actions I felt a slight movement coming from the tree and what followed thereafter kept me rooted in my spot. It seems that what I had feared just came to life and there it was all high and mighty.

"Who dared to awake Treebeard the Oldest Ent of Ents that exist from it's slumber?", It asked in a loud roaring tone.

On hearing that I had no idea whether it was my bravery or my stupidity that was voicing out. Perhaps it was rather the fact that I was glued to my spot with my entire body radiating a sense of fight or flight thus giving the cells within my brain a heads up and before I even realized the words had already escaped from my mouth.

"It was I and I apologize for doing so...", I trailed off with while being stunned at my own words.

"Oh Allah, what have I done!", I thought to myself. Did I just provoke it? On the thought of that I sneaked a peak at the so called Ent but what came after made me feel bewildered to such a point that I'm pretty sure would be the most understated feeling in the entire universe. There it stood the all high and mighty creature feared by all as read and heard in many stories with a bright smile on its' face stretching from ear to ear and a glow radiating off it in the most positive way possible. Who would have thought that a creature feared by most including I would have such a positive aura breathing through its' roots.

"Oh Child, it's just you! What a pleasant surprise!", said the Ent in its' old raspy voice.

"H-how do y-you know me? Ents only exist in fantasies and I have been dragged in to this realm I have no knowledge of.", I asked it in a state of shock. How does something that I have only read off in books say that it knows who I am. "Oh Allah, what is going on here. Why am I here and who am I?"

"Oh Child, I have existed for over millennium moons, these roots hear and feel everything. As far as you being here, that is all destiny's game my Child.", it stated in its' own wisely manner.

"D-destiny? What game is it playing with me?", I asked in a rather too blunt tone.

"Oh child, that is something you will have to unravel with the help of your friends. Choose your friends very wisely my child as not all are who we think they seem to be. Destiny is playing it's part my child, beware to play your part wisely. Only believe what feels true to the heart and do not go astray from the path that has chosen you! There is lots to learn on this journey yet my child. Always believe in yourself, you have been born to do many great things.", Treebeard boomed in its wisely tone.

With that said I turned around to look at my friends, Shahid, Leila, Luke and Commander Damien with a suspicious eye still rooted in my spot. I am still unable to comprehend the words uttered by Treebeard. What more is there for me to learn? All this new information is only brewing more questions. Questions that I doubt anyone has the answers to besides this so called destiny.

As I turn around back to ask Treebeard more questions I heard him whisper "It is time for me to return back to my slumber. Be wise my child and follow your heart.", this was then followed by a yawn sprawling from its mouth.

Hi guys

It's been a while since I have last updated but I'm back now with more adventure and I now present to you chapter 12. Well, well what have we here! It seems that Treebeard has some knowledge about Ayanna. What destiny is he talking off and where would it lead Ayanna to? What path has been chosen for her? Yet again Ayanna is made to question herself and yet again we have too many questions to pry the answers off but will destiny be able to answer them all. Till next time folks.

Sam

*****

Chapter 13

It has been two moons now since the incident with Treebeard and I have neither spoken to anyone about my thoughts nor have we as a group discussed anything that Treebeard had said. However we still continued the journey to the royal castle with as much precaution as possible.

Commander Damien keeps on glancing at me with weary eyes as though any second something will happen to me. It's frightening to know that creatures that exist in fantasy novels are more informed about my existence than myself. "Oh Allah, what has all this been reduced to. What is it that these creatures have knowledge of that I don't?"

"Oh Allah, I am in dire need of your guidance. Please show me the right path as you are the knower of all knowledge and the best of the best protector's." I voiced out my plea to Allah in my mind.

As I was still caught up in my thoughts I had not noticed that I was walking way ahead than everyone else until a dark figure stood in front of me. On realising that I looked up to see who it could be and at just one glance I felt my heart beating at an unimaginable speed. There he stood, my worst nightmare ever with a sinister smirk plastered on his face.Gythe, the very one that feeds on one's fear, and on realising that I tried to put on a brave mask of my own but Commander Damien had already strolled to us and had me covering behind him. Gythe instantly notices this and his sinister smirk widens even more. What does this all have to do with him.

"Well, well, if it isn't Commander Damien protecting the damsel in distress." Gythe seethes with sarcasm lacing his words.

"Watch your tongue Gythe! This is between you and I, there is no need to involve a mere human who does not even have the slightest knowledge of her own existence." Commander Damien roars out with fume brewing in him.

"Oh Damien, you and I are both aware that she is no mere human. There is certainly something special about her and I will surely get to the bottom of it." Gythe states with slyness spewing along with his words.

"Have I not warned you to let her be. Nevertheless to what have I been graced with your presence?", Commander Damien enquires as he gets even more irked by Gythes presence.

"Too much naiveness is beyond stupidity, Damien, or is it that you have forgotten your originality?", Gythe remarks attempting to fuel Commander Damien's anger.

"I am very well aware of my originality, I am Damien Salvador the fourth, Commander of the Royal Warrior Angels!", Commander Damien boomed getting furious by the minute.

"An Angel, is that what you want to become?", Gythe questions as though Commander Damien is not an Angel but rather a different species.

"I am already an Angel what more is there to be?" Commander Damien counters back.

"What about your other half? Have you remarkably forgotten your originality to such an extent that you no longer embrace it?", Gythe further questioned accusing Commander Damien's existence.

"Aah, my other half! A darkness that is bound to me to such an extent that it even lingers within the shadows.", Commander Damien states as the sudden realisation dawns upon him.

"Yes the very darkness, be warned it is awaiting your arrival! There is not many moons left. You can either embrace your originality or lose your existence. It is up to you now, choose wisely.", Gythe informed Commander Damien and with that he vanished in to a black smoke.

Gythe had left us all astonished. He had come to warn Commander Damien but why would he do that? Gythe is a Jin, they despise Angels to great ordeals yet he was here warning Commander Damien of his originality. What is it that is so harmful about Commander Damien's originality that a Jin had to come and warn him of it? Is Commander Damien not an Angel? Is there something far greater to his existence?

Oh Allah, all these new questions are brewing a headache. Why am I only getting more questions and not even a single answer to any of my other questions. It seem as though I am in a loop of questions where either mine or someone else's existence is questioned. I wonder what this so called destiny is hinting towards.

Hi guys

It seems a confused Ayanna has become even more confused with this profound information. What relationship does Commander Damien and Gythe share that led to Gythe's arrival and to warn him? What is this so called darkness being mentioned of? Is Commander Damien an Angel or is there something far greater to his existence? Yet another loop of questions that have no answer to them. Let's await and see how destiny plays its role and whether it can accommodate to all the brewing questions. Till next time folks.

Sam

*****

Chapter 14

Commander Damien's POV

As we continued our journey to the royal castle, Ayanna had been walking a bit ahead of us swirled within her own curiosity. Not much later I noticed that she had stopped walking and at seeing as to why she had stopped every fibre within me aroused with anger and hatred.

There he stood with a dark gloom encircling him and a sinister smirk plastered on his face. On seeing that I felt a sudden wave of protectiveness towards Ayanna and within split seconds I had her backed away behind me. Oh in the name of Angelea what is this great fondness and protectiveness that I feel towards Ayanna. Could this be my feelings of love towards her however before I could continue with my train of thoughts I was interrupted by Gythes' menacing voice. Yes Gythe the very one that had captured Ayanna and her friends nevertheless why is he here? Has he been following us?

"Well, well, if it isn't Commander Damien protecting the damsel in distress." Gythe seethes with sarcasm lacing his words.

"Watch your tongue Gythe! This is between you and I, there is no need to involve a mere human who does not even have the slightest knowledge of her own existence." I roar out with fume brewing within me.

Unfortunately yes, there is some history between Gythe and I but that is a discussion for a much later time. How dare he call her a damsel in distress, Ayanna is much powerful than she seems to showcase although that is not her fault as she is still unaware of her true self. She is no mere human and I can feel the power scorching through her nonetheless I had to state the opposite to get Gythe of her back. Ayanna is special unlike no other.

"Oh Damien, you and I are both aware that she is no mere human. There is certainly something special about her and I will surely get to the bottom of it." Gythe states with slyness spewing along with his words.

"Have I not warned you to let her be. Nevertheless to what have I been graced with your presence?", I enquire as Gythes' presence irks me even more.

"Too much naiveness is beyond stupidity, Damien, or is it that you have forgotten your originality?", Gythe remarks attempting to fuel my anger.

What originality is Gythe speaking off ? I am an Angel and that too a commander unless he is speaking of the change... No, that cannot be possible I am sure there is still many moons left for that unless I am wrong. No, I will not let this happen, I am Damien Salvador Commander of the Royal Warrior Angels! I need to regain myself and let Gythe know who I am.

"I am very well aware of my originality, I am Damien Salvador the fourth, Commander of the Royal Warrior Angels!", I boomed getting furious by the minute.

"An Angel, is that what you want to become?", Gythe yet again questions my originality as though I am not an Angel but rather a different species.

"I am already an Angel what more is there to be?" I counter back not yet coming to terms with what might lay ahead of me.

"What about your other half? Have you remarkably forgotten your originality to such an extent that you no longer embrace it?", Gythe further questions accusing my existence. It seems that my assumptions have been correct.

"Aah, my other half! A darkness that is bound to me to such an extent that it even lingers within the shadows.", I state as more realisation dawns upon me.

"Yes the very darkness, be warned it is awaiting your arrival! There is not many moons left. You can either embrace your originality or lose your existence. It is up to you now, choose wisely.", Gythe informs me however before I could even further question him about it he had already vanished into a black smoke.

It seems I have been wronged. I do not have many moons left but precisely how many moons do I have. I need to get Ayanna and her friends along with Luke to the Royal Castle as early as possible. I cannot let them witness this change or else their faith in me shall be lost forever. Oh in the name of Angelea guide me along what is righteous and protect me from the evilness of which I shall be encased in.

*****

Chapter 15

Leila's POV

It has been 3 days or what these so called creatures call moons since the appearance of Gythe and their confrontation with Commander Damien. Both Shahid and I are absolutely befuddled as to what is going on over here. First we find out that Ayanna is an Angel and now Commander Damien might be bipolar if such a thing even exists in this so called realm.

I am already petrified about my life after being kidnapped by Gythe and now this! Hold on, could this be connected to what Gythe had been speaking of when he had held me captured in that cave? Could all this be a conspiracy so that they can take over and spread evilness all over, even over Earth? Home, no they can't destroy it unless they find her? Who could she be? Well, who ever she was or is, she sounds very powerful as if she was part of some ancient legend... Oh well, who am I kidding this place in itself is ancient so what could be more legendary than this?

We have been constantly walking through this forest with minimum amount of sleep and rest ever since Gythe appeared. It seems as if Commander Damien has gone into some kind of panic mode as he is hell bent on getting us to the Royal Castle as soon as possible. What is he hiding so badly that he wants us to get off his back at the earliest? Could he be one of them as in a Jinn and is just pretending to be an Angel? Has he been fooling us all along and finally his mask is going to be removed? Well, if that was the case then I don't think he would have sworn his life into protecting us and Ayanna especially, however I might be wronged, who knows? Unfortunately, I don't know if the others have noticed but Commander Damien has officially made it to my list of suspicious people. Wait a second, scratch that it should rather be "suspicious creatures" as he is clearly not a human.

I have also noticed Commander Damien's growing fondness towards Ayanna. Has he been catching feelings for her? Oh boy, Ayanna you are surely trapped in one never ending roller-coaster! I truly feel sorry for you at such times. To be honest I actually kind of regret daring her to opening that book because just look at how things have turned out. Ayanna has gone ballistic about her identity, it's as if she no longer knows who she is. Just like a toddler learning and grasping new things about herself. I still however do not understand as to how she is an Angel. Was this all predestined by Allah or is there something else going on over here?

"Oh Allah, we are in dire need of your guidance, please give us some kind of sign so that we can at least have more faith that what ever is happening is happening for the best. We need to know whether we are on the right path or not.", I mentally prayed hoping that he somehow answers our prayers. I just need one sign however there are thousands of questions roaming around my mind. Oh boy, don't tell me that I'm becoming an over curious mind just like Ayanna! Oh well, when you have absolutely no cooking clue as to what is happening around you, you are bond to develop an over curious mind.

Speaking of curiosity, sure we have discovered that Ayanna is an Angel and that is why she was sucked into this realm but what does it have to do with Shahid and I. We are not Angels and nor do we have any powers. We are just ordinary humans unless Shahid might know something that we don't know, after all he is the oldest amongst the three of us. I'm sure he must know something that I don't know off! I will just have to wait and ask him later about it but I doubt he will tell me anything, nevertheless my eyes are currently set on Commander Damien. He has been acting way too suspicious and I'm beginning to loose my trust in him, however most importantly we all need to be safe. Oh, how I miss home! I just wish all this can end as soon as possible. I really miss my family back at home and I hope we would be able to go back and not be stuck in here forever.

Chapter 16

It has been three moons since Gythe made his appearance causing everyone to be on edge. However, instead of being preoccupied about the thoughts of my wellbeing as well as that of my friends and the reason behind me being an angel, my mind is running wild in an endless loop of thoughts on the words spoken by Gythe.

There surely has to be some explanation behind his words but the fact that Commander Damien is hell bent on getting us to the Royal Castle as soon as possible does not really give much help to the situation. We have been constantly walking through this forest with minimum amount of sleep and rest along with Commander Damien panicking every now and then. I did not think Gythe's words would have such an effect on him, nevertheless Commander Damien is the leader of the Warrior Angels, I'm sure he has experienced such situations in the past, then why is he so fazed by it? What could he possibly be hiding from us?

Gythe had mentioned about Commander Damien's other half... What or who could this other half be? Well, it certainly cannot be another person as it is bound to him to such an extent that it even lingers within the shadows. What is it that is so harmful and malevolent about his originality that it has struck him with such trepidation? Cou - could he be what I think he might be? I-i have read of many books in which different races more like different types of creatures have mixed together creating a new and advanced race, so could it be possible that Commander Damien might be a hybrid, half Angel and half Jinn? No, no, it cannot be! He had clearly stated that he is an Angel and had sworn to protect my friends and I with his life. All this while I have never seen nor felt an ounce of evilness radiating of him, than how could it be possible? It just does not add up. There has to be another reason to all of this, I can feel it!

"Oh Allah, what is this feeling that constantly ignites within me at the very mention of his name?" Sure, I am aware of the fact that I am attracted to him, but this... This feeling is far greater than just an attraction. It is as if it is not a feeling of sparks but rather an invisible rope bonding us while we remain at the ends of it. How come I had not felt this before or perhaps I had not taken the time to acknowledge and neither get involved within the depths of my feelings and emotions towards Commander Damien. However, I cannot neglect them any longer as his actions continue to thrive my feelings for him further resulting in something I had never expected of occurring and that too this soon. It is time, I accept these feelings and allow it to blossom into something magnificent and majestic. It is time, I accept these emotions of love towards him that only wish to protect him from the evilness that incases us as he has been protecting me all along, while destiny plays its parts to an unknown future.

Oh destiny, I have no idea why you desired to drag me into a world I have no knowledge of. A world where I am not who I was brought up to be but rather to seek out that my existence was all a lie. I was deceived of my originality and still have no indication of where it all might lead too, yet there is Commander Damien who was aware of his originality but chose to forget it. Now it is the very thing that is haunting him, giving him another chance at rectifying his mistake. I hope he makes the right decision. Oh destiny, what kind of a play is this, but you better be playing your cards right as I have already smelt malevolence before I even entered this so called play of yours.

"Look there is the castle, we have almost reached it.", Luke stated, ending my repelling thoughts of what destiny has lead us to.

"Wow" is the only word that I could think of as I gasped at the beauty of the castle. There it stood in all its white glory. I wonder what its inside would behold when the outside of it is quite magical and intrancing.

"Well, what are we waiting for then. Let's get going, we need to find answers to all that is happening." Shahid said in an attempt to motivate us.

With that said we set off on our way to the Royal Castle, hoping that who ever resides there will have some sort of answers to all our questions and perhaps let us in on what destiny has in-store for us.